Beware of the Storybook Wolves

Lauren Child

SCHOLASTIC INC.

New York Toronto London Auckland Sydney
Mexico City New Delhi Hong Kong Buenos Aires

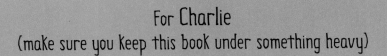

For Charlie
(make sure you keep this book under something heavy)

and Cress
(who knows how to deal with storybook wolves)

Thank you to Soren

Arthur A. Levine Books hardcover edition published by Arthur A. Levine Books, an imprint of Scholastic Press, May 2001

ISBN 0-439-35236-3

Copyright © 2000 by Lauren Child.
All rights reserved.
Published by Scholastic Inc., by arrangement with Hodder Children's Books. SCHOLASTIC, the LANTERN LOGO, and associated logos are trademarks and/or registered trademarks of Scholastic Inc.

12 11 10 9 8 7 6 5 4 3 2   1 2 3 4 5 6/0

Printed in the U.S.A.   08

First Scholastic paperback printing, September 2001

Little Red Riding Hood

Every night Herb's mother would read him a bedtime story.
Sometimes it was about a big wolf who terrified little girls and their
grandmothers with his chilling growl and his big yellow teeth. You could tell
from the picture that toothpaste had never been on his shopping list.

The story got very nasty in the middle and everybody nearly came to a
sticky end ... but, by the last page ...

...it had all turned out
well and went
happy-ever-afterly.

It was one of
Herb's favorites.
He particularly liked
the back cover which had
a picture of a smaller
wolf with a patch over
one eye and the words:

For a real thrill, try reading the story of
THE LITTLE FIERCE WOLF
AND THE THREE PINK PIGLETS
It will scare your socks off.

Whenever his mother finished this bedtime story, Herb would say, "Don't forget to take that book with you!"
And his mother would ask, "Why?"
"Because there's a wolf in it, of course," Herb would say.

Herb's mother would smile to herself because she knew that storybook wolves are not at all dangerous.

One night, just as they were finishing the
wolf story, the telephone rang.
In her hurry, Herb's mother forgot all
about taking the book with her.

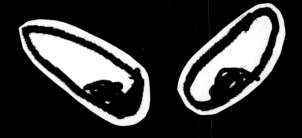

Herb didn't
realize at first
but, as he was
snoozing off, he
thought he
heard a deep
rumbling sound
coming from his
bedside table.

It was like the rumbling of a very hungry tummy. Or perhaps even two very hungry tummies.

Then he began to smell a not-very-nice smell. A sort of bad-breath type of a smell. Herb got a funny feeling that two, or maybe even three, eyes were watching him.

Unwisely, he switched on the light . . .

Little Red Riding Hood

. . . and there, standing in front of him, was the **big storybook wolf** and next to him was the other **smaller wolf** with a patch over one eye (Herb recognized him as the back-cover wolf).

"Mmm," Big Wolf said in a low greedy voice, "**I thought I could smell something tasty. I'm going to gobble you up, little boy.**" And he started to lick his chops.

"**Ooh, can I have his little pink toes? They look just like piglets,**" said Little Wolf.

And he tried to lick his chops,
but he wasn't very good at it and just
ended up dribbling on the carpet.

"I wouldn't eat me yet," stammered
Herb, desperately trying to think
of a plan to distract the wolves
from wolfing him down.
"Why not?" said Big Wolf, giving
him a sideways stare.
"Yes, why not?" said Little Wolf,
trying to give him a sideways stare.

"Ummm ... because little boys are
for dessert. You have to start
with appetizers, of course."
'I didn't know that,' said Big Wolf.
"Really?" said Herb, feeling a little bit
pleased with his own craftiness.
"I thought everybody knew that."
'Oh, I knew that,' said Little Wolf.
'No, you did not,' said Big
slightly-less-fierce-than-before Wolf.
'Yes, I certainly did,' said
Little Wolf, puffing himself up.
'Well, if you're so clever,
then what's 'appetizers'?'
triumphed Big Wolf.

You could tell that Little Wolf hadn't even heard of appetizers but, not wishing to sound stupid, he shouted, **'Jell-O is an appetizer! Everybody knows that.'**

Then Big Wolf and Little Wolf looked at Herb and said, **'Where's the Jell-O?'**

Jell-O, Jell-O, where was the Jell-O?

Herb's mind was whirring like a frantic thing.

Then he caught sight of his book of fairy tales.

He had been looking at it last night and it was lying open on the page where the dozy princess falls asleep at her own birthday party.

No one at the table would notice if he borrowed some Jell-O. They were all snoozing, tired of waiting for *Princess Beautiful* to wake up.

Herb was so busy struggling to slide the Jell-O off the page he didn't notice the wicked fairy, wide awake and hiding under the table. She had been listening to every word. This was bad luck for Herb because the wicked fairy hated little boys only slightly less than she hated little girls. They made her very nervous. She'd seen what those little brats Hansel and Gretel had done to that poor defenseless witch. Not only did they nibble her cottage half to pieces, but then they went and shoved her in her own oven. Children put her in a very bad mood indeed.

"Oh, you dozy doormats, don't you know anything?" snarled the fairy. "You wolf-halfwits give wickedness a bad name. He's tricked you, you twerps:

Little boys are appetizers, Jell-O is dessert."

And with that, the wicked fairy jumped back into the book and snapped it shut.

First the wolves went almost purple in the cheeks with embarrassment, then their eyes went all mean and squinty.

Herb could tell things had taken a turn for the really quite bad. So he snatched up the fairy-tale book, found the page with the Fairy Godmother, and shook it until she tumbled out of the book and onto the floor. She was a bit cross actually because her dress got crumpled and she nearly twisted her ankle. "Well," she said, "I've got a good mind to turn you into a caterpillar, little boy."

"No, no!" said Herb. "Don't turn me into a caterpillar. It's those two who need to be caterpillars."

"Oh no, not you two again," said the Godmother, spying the two alarmed wolves. "Always making trouble... blowing people's houses down and gobbling them up without so much as a do-you-mind."

As she said this, she accidentally waved her wand at the little wolf
and the smoke went *poof* (just like in the fairy tales) and suddenly
there was the little wolf standing in a ballgown.

"Oh dear, oh dear, this will never do," said the Fairy Godmother,
shaking her head. "That dress was meant for Cinderella. You
shook me out of the book just as I was about to send her to the
ball. Awfully nice dress though. I have an eye for fashion
as you can probably tell. But not at all suitable for a wolf."

Little Wolf took one look in the mirror and was so pleased with his new look that he jumped into the fairy-tale book and went to the ball himself.

Which of course left Cinderella having a night in,
cleaning the kitchen after all.

"Oh well, that's that then," sighed the Fairy Godmother. "I'm not going to be at all popular at the palace now. I don't know what the king and queen are going to say when a wolf turns up at the ball to dance with their son. I imagine they will be very grumpy about it. I do hope he doesn't start snacking on the guests. . . ."

The Fairy Godmother was
so engrossed with her own
problems that she hadn't
noticed that Big Wolf
was poised, ready
to swallow Herb
in one gulp.

"Help!"

screeched Herb.

Quick as a quick thing, the Fairy Godmother whooshed her wand
and Big Wolf became a tiny caterpillar.

"Oh, I do like caterpillars," said the Fairy Godmother, popping it back into the wolf storybook. "They're so undemanding. Never bothering me for things, not like frogs, always thinking they are princes. What's more, I really have had enough of being squashed inside a book, doing favors for spoiled princesses. I'm going to take a vacation, somewhere far away from royalty."

And in a sudden twinkle of sequins, she disappeared.

Before Herb got back into bed, he piled
up all his books and then put the
heaviest thing he could find on top of
them, just in case anyone else was
tempted to get out of his story.

Then he switched off his light aND DREAMED of fierce CATERPILLARS, fashionable wolves, and grouchy godmothers.

The funny thing was, the next time Herb's mother came to read the wolf story, there was no wolf to be seen — just a tiny caterpillar trying with all his might to terrify a little girl in a red coat.